JIM, THE CAT

by Jean Poindexter Colby

Pictures by Marie C. Nichols

JC6727j

LITTLE, BROWN AND COMPANY · BOSTON · TORONTO

Published simultaneously in Canada
by Little, Brown & Company (Canada) Limited

PRINTED IN THE UNITED STATES OF AMERICA

JIM, THE CAT

Jim was a thin raggedy tiger kitten with very long whiskers. He first appeared in the Holdens' garden one cold wet spring day when Lucy was gloomily sitting in the swing in her snow suit. She had been very sick that winter and the doctor had said, "Keep her out of school. See that she gets plenty of fresh air. Fatten her up."

"I don't want fresh air. I don't want to be fattened up," said Lucy. But she tried to eat the liver and drink the milk her mother kept serving her. And she bundled up every day and went outdoors even when it was cold and blowy and there was nothing to do outside and no one to do it with.

So she was delighted to see Jim even though he was thin as a piece of cardboard and just about as pretty.

"Here kitty, come kitty," she called gently.

Jim backed away. Human beings had not been kind to him and he was suspicious even of this small-sized one.

Lucy thought of the graham cracker she was supposed to eat in ten minutes. She fished it out of her pocket and held it toward him. "Come, kitty," she called again.

Jim had just ventured a little closer when the back door opened and Lucy's mother called out, "Come in, dear. Time for your glass of milk."

At that the kitten bounded off into the bushes.

"Oh, Mother, you scared him." Lucy's voice showed her disappointment as she scuffed slowly toward the house.

"Scared whom?" asked her mother.

"The kitty. A little kitty came to see me just now. A thin funny-looking kitty. I don't want any milk, Mother. I just can't drink it."

"Oh, there he is." Lucy's mother spied Jim in the bushes. "He *is* thin and funny-looking." Suddenly she had an idea. "How would you like to share your milk with him? Would you drink half of it if he drank half?"

"Yes. That is if I can get him near enough. Are the dogs penned up?" Mr. Holden raised and trained pointers as a business.

"They're off with your father. You call the kitten while I bring a saucer," said Mrs. Holden.

By the time her mother reappeared Lucy had coaxed the kitten almost up to the back steps. She took off her mittens, and was pouring some of the milk into the saucer when the sun came out.

"Goodness, how wonderful! That's the first sun this month!" Mrs. Holden exclaimed.

Lucy looked up with practically her first smile that month. "The kitty brought the sun, Mother. I'm going to call him Sunny. How's that for a name, Mother?"

Mrs. Holden looked at the poor wisp of fur. "Well, he doesn't look the part now, but no matter. When I was a little girl I used to read a comic strip called 'Sunny Jim.' How would that be?"

"Oh, that's perfect, Mother! Here, Sunny. Here, Jim. See, either name works." For the kitten had run straight toward the saucer and was lapping up the milk as fast as he could.

"Now it's your turn," prompted Mother. And, sure enough, Lucy took her cup and drank her share.

In a moment there was the sound of a car in the drive and the barking of dogs. "Oh, Mother, the dogs will get Jim. What shall I do to save him?"

But Jim saved himself by streaking for a nearby tree and climbing out of reach just as two pointers tore around the corner, saw the kitten, and raced after him.

Mr. Holden appeared soon afterward. "Hello, Lucy. What's the excitement? I hope you drank your milk better today than yesterday."

"Oh, Daddy, I did. I mean half of it. Look, Daddy, it's a kitten—up the tree. I want to keep it, Daddy. Please call the dogs off."

Mr. Holden looked at Jim flattened against the branch. "You want to keep a cat? And especially a cat like that?" He sounded as if he could not believe his ears.

"Bert, wait a moment." Mrs. Holden had come out again on the back steps. "She just wants a pet."

"She wants a pet," Mr. Holden shouted, "with two full-blooded pointers in the family?"

"But they aren't mine," explained Lucy, "and they're so big anyway."

"May is going to have her puppies soon. You can have one of those," her father offered. "They ought to be beautiful dogs—the best full-blooded stock in this country."

"I don't want any full-blooded stock," cried Lucy tearfully. "I don't want a puppy that has to go to shows and be trained and can't live in the house. I just want Sunny Jim—" And with a burst of tears she ran into the house.

"And who is Sunny Jim?" asked Mr. Holden in disgust. "That *thing?*" He nodded at the little tiger cat, who at this point lost hold of the branch and dropped to the ground.

Mrs. Holden shouted this time, for both dogs bounded forward, intent on their tiny prey.

"Down, May! Down, Gordon!" But it wasn't Mr. Holden's voice that stopped the dogs. It was Sunny Jim himself as he wheeled around fast to face them, his tiny back up, his fur—what he had of it—out straight, and his little mouth spitting like an atomizer.

Both pointers backed off, and May, the female, even began to wag her tail a little.

"Well, how do you like that! Game little thing, isn't it!" Mr. Holden admitted, surprised. "But we can't have a cat. I wouldn't give one houseroom."

"Now, Bert . . ." And Mrs. Holden told him how Lucy had found the kitten and drunk her milk and acted so much more alive since Jim's arrival. "I think the kitty would do Lucy good. Let's just try keeping him, for a while anyway."

Mr. Holden gave in reluctantly. "All right, we'll try it, but if that cat harms May's puppies, I'll shoot it."

"He won't. I know you're afraid to let any animal around them for fear of germs or an accident, but poor little Jim is different. Aren't you, Jim?" And Mrs. Holden scooped him up carefully to take inside to Lucy.

In this way Jim was placed on trial in the Holden house. The first few days he was no trouble. In fact, he was practically invisible to everyone but Lucy. Whenever anyone else came in the room he dived under the sofa or bed or whatever was handy. And he stayed there until the other person went out.

Lucy loved him and immediately took a turn for the better. She seemed to be eating unusually large meals, but one day Mrs. Holden discovered the reason. She had just put a plate of fried liver in front of the little girl for luncheon and left the room, when she had to return unexpectedly. She was just in time to see a piece of the meat disappear under the table. She pushed the tablecloth aside and there was Jim, swallowing and licking his chops. Startled, for a quick moment he fixed his eyes on her, then sped across the hall and under the sofa.

Mrs. Holden knew enough not to be cross. "Don't we feed Jim enough?" she asked Lucy, whose face was very red.

"Yes, Mother, I'm sorry. I should have told you but I thought if I needed liver, Jim did too. Only yesterday the milkman said we were both thin and mangy-looking."

"Do you eat any of the meat yourself?"

"Oh yes, every other piece. Just the way you had us drink the milk the first day. Is that so bad of me?"

Mrs. Holden looked at her daughter, who was beginning to show the first signs of health in a long time. "No, but next time let's talk it over." Lucy agreed. "And from now on, we'll have two plates of liver."

It almost seemed as if Jim heard and understood. For once he squeezed out from under the sofa and walked toward Mrs. Holden, his tail straight and proud.

From that day on Jim was friends with Lucy's mother, but he still kept away from Mr. Holden. He spent most of the time outdoors with Lucy, whom he followed around like a dog. Or he was up on her bed when she was resting or sleeping. He loved to push himself under the pillow or the spread, hunting for imaginary enemies. He also loved to play with a spool that Lucy would drag on the end of a string.

One night Mr. Holden tripped on this string and growled and mumbled in the darkness. He groped around for the electric-light switch but Mrs. Holden ran downstairs and snapped it on before he did.

"It's that cat," he spluttered. "This house is like an obstacle race. I just can't stand it."

"I know, dear. You're worried about the puppies. I'm sure they'll be all right. They'll come soon, won't they?"

"Tonight, I expect. So put that cat out of here, will you? I don't want him around if I have to bring them in to the kitchen."

Mrs. Holden gently but firmly set Jim outside the door, and Lucy, who was watching over the banister, went sadly into her room. Tonight she would have to sleep alone. Perhaps every night from now on. It would be so lonely.

She had just settled down in bed and started to have a good cry when she heard a mewing outside her window. Rushing to look out into the darkness, she saw a pair of yellow eyes, and white whiskers. Jim had climbed up the rose trellis and was sitting on the window sill! And when she lifted him quietly inside, he seemed none the worse for his brief journey in the moonlight.

35

That night May had her puppies, and Mr. Holden was too busy the next few days to wonder what had happened to the kitten. They were beautiful puppies, seven in all, and even Lucy was tempted when her father offered to give her one of them. But she said, "No, Daddy, thank you. You know you will only sell them sometime and anyway I like Jim better."

Her father snorted in disgust. "So he's come back again. Well, see that he doesn't turn up around those puppies!"

Some time after that the family was eating dinner when they heard a great yelping in the kennel. Mr. Holden rushed out and came back shortly, holding one of the puppies to him. Its ear was streaming blood from a sharp bite near the head.

Just at that moment Jim hove in sight. Mr. Holden in his distress thought the cat was to blame. "Look at that animal! See, there is blood on its jaws! He's ruined a two-hundred-dollar puppy!"

"But, Daddy, he's just been eating liver, like me," Lucy defended. "Today we gave it to him raw. He wouldn't touch the puppy."

"She's right, Bert," agreed Mrs. Holden. "It's those rats again. You remember the trouble we had with them before. Let me see that ear. If I put a Band-Aid on that cut and draw it together I believe it will heal."

"Never," replied Mr. Holden. "He's marred for life. Wait until I see that cat again . . ."

But he never did. Jim continued to disappear whenever Mr. Holden came in sight, and peace reigned for a week or so.

Again they were eating dinner when the dogs began barking and yapping. All the family hurried out. This time Mr. Holden had his gun in one hand.

Lucy's heart sank when she saw Jim right in the middle of the outside wire kennel by the feeding station. His white vest stood out clearly in the evening light.

Lucy's father raised the gun to his shoulder.

"Daddy, don't!" Lucy cried.

But the man lowered the gun without firing. "Well, I'll be switched," he said slowly. "Look what that cat had in its mouth."

Now Lucy could see that the gray form at Jim's feet was not a puppy but a huge rat. Jim had bitten through the back of its neck and it was dead. But in the tussle, Jim, like the puppy, had been badly bitten in the ear.

This time Mr. Holden walked back to the house carefully carrying—of all things—Jim, the cat!

"Good dog," he murmured. "I mean, good cat. Brave cat. Fine cat. You've a home here for as long as you want."

So Jim became a full-time member of the Holden family. He seemed to sense his new importance and stalked daily through all the rooms of the house as if he owned them. He didn't even disappear at the sight of strangers any more. Instead he would leap up beside the bust of Shakespeare in the library and look over the newcomers very carefully.

"It's hard to tell who looks wiser, Jim or Shake-speare," said Mr. Holden as the doorbell rang one afternoon and the cat took up his lofty perch beside the poet.

It was the doctor this time, come to give Lucy a final examination before the Holdens left for a summer on the Maine coast.

"Tell us now if she isn't all right," said Mr. Holden firmly. "We're miles from a doctor up there."

The doctor listened to Lucy's chest, took her blood pressure, pricked her ear for a blood sample, looked down her throat and into her ears. Finally he had her step on the scales.

"Fit as a fiddle," he pronounced. "A tremendous improvement. How do you account for it?"

"Sunny Jim," spoke up Lucy. "But am I all well?" she asked. "Don't you think he had better come with me?"

"Now let me see," the doctor replied very seriously. He looked around at Jim, who had followed them into the bedroom and was now stretched out on the bed watching every move. "He looks better too. In fact I think he is going to be a handsome cat."

Lucy started to sputter because to her Jim was handsome already.

"Now wait a moment, my dear," the doctor continued. "He still could stand improvement, I think. I'm going to prescribe a summer in Maine for him. And, of course, you will have to go along to take care of him!"

Jim looked at the man with his big yellow eyes.
Then he closed one eye and opened it. Some people
might say he winked at the doctor. Or did he?